Dulce Domum

from
The Wind in the Willows

Written by
KENNETH GRAHAME

Abridged and illustrated by
INGA MOORE

TED SMART

Dulce Domum

The sheep ran huddling together against the hurdles, blowing out thin nostrils and stamping with delicate forefeet, their heads thrown back and a light steam rising from the crowded sheep-pen into the frosty air, as the two animals hastened by in high spirits. They were returning across country after a day's outing with Otter, and the shades of the short winter day were closing in. They had heard the sheep and had made for them; and now, leading from the sheep-pen, they found a beaten track.

"It looks as if we're coming to a village," said the Mole, slackening his pace.

"O, at this season of the year," said the Rat, "they're safe indoors by this time, men, women, children and all. We shall slip through without any bother."

The rapid nightfall of mid-December had quite beset the little village as they approached it on soft feet over a first thin fall of powdery snow. Little was visible but squares of a dusky orange-red on either side of the street, where the firelight or lamplight of each cottage overflowed through the casements into the dark world without. Most of the low latticed windows were innocent of blinds, and moving from one to another, the lookers-in, so far from home themselves, watched a cat being stroked, a sleepy child picked up and huddled off to bed, or a tired man stretch and knock out his pipe on the end of a smouldering log.

But it was from one little window, with its blind drawn down, that the sense of home most pulsated. Against the blind hung a bird-cage, clearly silhouetted. On the perch, the fluffy occupant, head tucked well into feathers, seemed so near to them as to be easily stroked, had they tried. As they looked, the sleepy little fellow stirred, shook himself, and raised his head. They could see the gape of his tiny beak as he yawned in a bored sort of way, looked around, and settled again. Then a gust of bitter wind took them in the back of the neck, a small sting of frozen sleet woke them as from a dream, and they knew their toes to be cold and their legs tired, and their own home distant a weary way.

Once beyond the village, they could smell the friendly fields again; and they braced themselves for the last long stretch, the home stretch, the stretch that we know is bound to end in the rattle of the door-latch, sudden firelight, and the sight of familiar things greeting us. They plodded along steadily and silently, each of them thinking his own thoughts. The Mole's ran a good deal on supper, as it was pitch dark, and it was all strange country to him as far as he knew. The Rat was walking a little way ahead, his eyes fixed on the road in front of him; so he did not notice Mole when the summons reached him, and took him like an electric shock.

We have only the word "smell" for the whole range of delicate thrills which murmur in the nose of the animal night and day. It was one of these mysterious fairy calls that suddenly reached Mole in the darkness, making him tingle through and through. He stopped dead in his tracks, his nose searching hither and thither.

Home! That was what they meant, those soft touches wafted through the air, those invisible little hands pulling and tugging, all one way! Why, it must be quite close by him at that moment, his old home he had forsaken when he first found the river! Since that bright morning he had hardly given it a thought. Shabby and poorly furnished, and yet his, the home he had made for himself, the home he had been so happy to get back to after his day's work. And the home was missing him, and wanted him back, and was telling him so, through his nose, sorrowfully, but with no bitterness or anger; that it was there, and wanted him.

"Ratty!" he called. "Come back! I want you, quick!"

"O, *come* along, Mole!" replied the Rat, plodding along.

"Stop, Ratty!" pleaded the Mole. "You don't understand! It's my home, my old home! I've just come across the smell of it, and it's really quite close. Come back, Ratty! Please!"

The Rat was by this time very far ahead, too far to hear what the Mole was calling.

"We mustn't stop now!" he called back. "It's late, and the snow's coming on again, and I'm not sure of the way! And I want your nose, Mole, so come on, there's a good fellow!" And the Rat pressed on without waiting for an answer.

Poor Mole stood alone in the road, his heart torn asunder, a big sob gathering, somewhere low down inside him. Never for a moment did he dream of abandoning his friend. His old home pleaded, whispered. With a wrench he followed in the track of the Rat, while faint, thin little smells, still dogging his nose, reproached him for his forgetfulness.

He caught up the Rat, who began chattering about what they would do when they got back, and how jolly a fire in the parlour would be, and what a supper he meant to eat; never noticing his companion's silence. At last, when they were passing some tree-stumps at the edge of a copse, he stopped and said kindly, "Look here, Mole, old chap, you seem dead tired. No talk left in you, and your feet dragging like lead. We'll sit down here for a minute and rest. The snow has held off, and the best part of our journey is over."

The Mole tried to control himself, for he felt it coming, the sob he had fought so long. Up and up, it forced its way to the air, and then another, and another, and others thick and fast; till poor Mole at last gave up the struggle, and cried helplessly, now that he knew it was all over and he had lost what he could hardly be said to have found.

The Rat did not dare to speak for a while. At last he said, "What is it, old fellow? Whatever can be the matter?"

Mole found it difficult to get any words out. "I know it's a – shabby, little place," he sobbed at last: "not like – your cosy quarters – or Toad's beautiful hall – or Badger's great house – but it was my own little home – and I was fond of it – and then I smelt it suddenly – on the road, when I called and you wouldn't listen, Rat. – We might have just gone and had one look at it – but you wouldn't turn back, you wouldn't!"

The Rat stared in front of him, saying nothing. After a time he muttered, "What a *pig* I have been! A *pig* – that's me!"

Then he rose, and, remarking, "Well, we'd better be getting on!" set off up the road again, the way they had come.

"Wherever are you (hic) going to, Ratty?" cried the Mole.

"We're going to find that home of yours, old fellow," replied the Rat pleasantly.

"Come back, Ratty, do!" cried the Mole, hurrying after him. "The snow's coming! Think of River Bank, and your supper!"

"Hang River Bank!" said the Rat heartily. When it seemed they must be nearing that part of the road where the Mole had been "held up", Rat said, "Now! Use your nose!"

Mole stood a moment rigid. His uplifted nose, quivering slightly, felt the air.

Then a short, quick run forward – a fault – a check – a try back; and then a slow, steady, confident advance.

The Rat kept close to his heels as the Mole, with something of the air of a sleep-walker, crossed a dry ditch, scrambled through a hedge, and nosed his way over a field open and trackless and bare in the faint starlight.

Suddenly he dived; the Rat promptly followed him down the tunnel to which his unerring nose had faithfully led him.

It was close and airless, and the earthy smell was strong. The Mole struck a match, and by its light the Rat saw that they were standing in an open space, neatly swept and sanded underfoot, and directly facing them was Mole's little front door, with "Mole End" painted, in Gothic lettering, over the bell-pull at the side.

Mole reached down a lantern from a nail on the wall and lit it, and the Rat, looking round him, saw that they were in a sort of fore-court. A garden-seat stood on one side of the door, and on the other, a roller; for the Mole, who was a tidy animal, could not stand having his ground kicked up into earth-heaps. On the walls hung wire baskets with ferns in them, brackets carrying plaster statuary – Garibaldi, and the infant Samuel, and Queen Victoria, and other heroes of modern Italy. Down one side of the fore-court ran a skittle-alley, with benches along it and little wooden tables. In the middle was a small pond containing goldfish and surrounded by a cockle-shell border. Out of the centre of the pond rose a fanciful erection clothed in more cockle-shells and topped by a large silvered glass ball that reflected everything all wrong and had a very pleasing effect.

Mole's face beamed at the sight of all these objects so dear to him, and he hurried Rat through the door, lit a lamp in the hall, and took one glance round his old home. He saw the dust lying thick on everything, saw the cheerless, deserted look of the long-neglected house, and its worn and shabby contents – and collapsed again on a hall-chair, his nose in his paws.

"O, Ratty!" he cried dismally, "why ever did I do it? Why did I bring you to this poor, cold place, when you might have been at River Bank, with all your nice things about you!"

The Rat was running here and there, opening doors, and cupboards; lighting lamps and candles and sticking them up everywhere. "What a capital little house this is!" he called out cheerily. "We'll make a jolly night of it. The first thing we want is a good fire; I'll see to that. You get a duster, Mole, and try and smarten things up a bit."

Encouraged by his companion, the Mole roused himself and dusted with energy, while the Rat soon had a cheerful blaze roaring up the chimney. But Mole had another fit of the blues, dropping on a couch and burying his face in his duster.

"Rat," he moaned, "you poor, hungry, animal. I've nothing to give you – nothing – not a crumb!"

"What a fellow you are for giving in!" said the Rat. "Why, only just now I saw a sardine-opener on the kitchen dresser, quite distinctly; and everybody knows that means there are sardines about somewhere. Come with me and forage."

They went hunting through every cupboard and drawer. The result was not so depressing after all, though of course it might have been better; a tin of sardines – a box of captain's biscuits, nearly full – and a German sausage in silver paper.

The Rat busied himself fetching plates, knives and forks, and mustard which he mixed in an egg-cup, and had just got seriously to work with the sardine-opener when sounds were heard from the fore-court without – like the scuffling of small feet in the gravel and a murmur of tiny voices – "All in a line – hold the lantern up a bit, Tommy – no coughing after I say one, two, three. – Come on, we're all a-waiting—"

"What's up?" inquired the Rat.

"I think it must be the field-mice," replied the Mole, with a touch of pride in his manner. "They go round carol-singing regularly at this time of year. They're quite an institution in these parts. And they never pass me over – they come to Mole End last of all; and I used to give them hot drinks, and supper too sometimes, when I could afford it. It will be like old times to hear them again."

"Let's have a look at them!" cried the Rat, jumping up and running to the door.

In the fore-court, lit by the dim rays of a horn lantern, some eight or ten little field-mice stood in a semicircle, red worsted comforters round their throats, their fore-paws thrust deep into their pockets, their feet jigging for warmth. With bright beady eyes they glanced shyly at each other, sniggering a little, sniffing and applying coat-sleeves a good deal.

As the door opened, their shrill little voices uprose on the air.

Carol

Villagers all, this frosty tide,
Let your doors swing open wide,
Though wind may follow,
*   and snow beside,*
Yet draw us in by your fire to bide;
Joy shall be yours in the morning!

Here we stand in the cold and sleet,
Blowing fingers and stamping feet,
Come from far away you to greet –
You by the fire and we in the street –
Bidding you joy in the morning!

"Well sung!" cried the Rat. "And now come along in, all of you, and have something hot!"

"Yes, come along, field-mice," cried the Mole eagerly. "You just wait a minute, while we – O, Ratty!" he cried in despair. "Whatever are we doing? We've nothing to give them!"

"You leave all that to me," said the Rat. "Here, you with the lantern! Are there any shops open at this hour of the night?"

"Certainly, sir," replied the field-mouse respectfully. "At this time of year our shops keep open to all sorts of hours."

"Then you go off at once," said the Rat, "and get me—"

Here the Mole only heard "Fresh, mind! – no, a pound will do – only the best – if you can't get it there, try somewhere else – of course, home-made, no tinned stuff – well, do the best you can!" There was a chink of coin passing from paw to paw, the field-mouse was provided with a basket for his purchases, and off he hurried, he and his lantern.

The rest of the field-mice perched in a row on the settle, their small legs swinging.

"They act plays too," the Mole explained to the Rat. "Make them up all by themselves. They gave us a capital one last year, about a field-mouse who was captured at sea and made to row in a galley; and when he escaped and got home, his lady-love had gone into a convent. Here, you were in it, I remember. Get up and recite a bit."

The field-mouse addressed got up on his legs, giggled shyly, looked round the room, and remained absolutely tongue-tied. His comrades cheered him on, Mole coaxed him, but nothing could overcome his stage-fright. Then the door opened, and the field-mouse with the lantern reappeared, staggering under the weight of his basket.

In a few minutes supper was ready, and Mole, as he took the head of the table, saw his little friends' faces brighten and beam as they fell to and thought what a happy home-coming this had turned out, after all. As they ate, they talked of old times,

and the field-mice gave him the local gossip up to date, and answered as well as they could the hundred questions he had to ask them. The Rat said little or nothing, only taking care that each guest had what he wanted, and plenty of it, and that Mole had no trouble or anxiety about anything.

They clattered off at last, with their jacket pockets stuffed with remembrances for the small brothers and sisters at home. When the door had closed on the last of them and the chink of the lanterns had died away, Mole and Rat kicked the fire up, drew their chairs in, and discussed the events of the long day. At last the Rat, with a tremendous yawn, said, "Mole, old chap, I'm ready to drop. Sleepy is simply not the word. That your own bunk over on that side? Very well, then, I'll take this. What a ripping little house this is! Everything so handy!"

He clambered into his bunk and rolled himself well up in the blankets, and slumber gathered him forthwith.

The weary Mole also soon had his head on his pillow. But ere he closed his eyes he let them wander round his old room, mellow in the glow of the firelight that played on familiar and friendly things. He saw clearly how plain and simple – how narrow, even – it all was; but clearly, too, how much it all meant to him. He did not at all want to abandon the new life, to turn his back on sun and air; the upper world was all too strong, it called to him still, even down there, and he knew he must return. But it was good to think he had this to come back to, this place which was all his own, these things which were so glad to see him again and could always be counted upon for the same simple welcome.